ENERGY EVERYWHERE

SPEEDING! MECHANICAL ENERGY

Emma Carlson Berne

PowerKiDS press
New York

Published in 2013 by The Rosen Publishing Group, Inc.
29 East 21st Street, New York, NY 10010

First Edition

Editor: Jennifer Way
Book Design: Andrew Povolny

Photo Credits: Cover Calvin Chan/Shutterstock.com; p. 4 Racheal Grazias/Shutterstock.com; p. 5 I hope you'll like it/Flickr/Getty Images; p. 6 D. Sharon Pruitt Pink Sherbet Photography/Flickr/Getty Images; p. 7 Jupiterimages/Brand X Pictures/Getty Images; pp. 8–9 KKulikov/Shutterstock.com; p. 10 tr3gin/Shutterstock.com; p. 11 © www.iStockphoto.com/Dieter Spears; p. 12 Angelo Giampicciolo/Shutterstock.com; p. 13 (top) William Attard McCarthy/Shutterstock.com; p. 13 (bottom) Gaby Saliba/Shutterstock.com; p. 14 Jen Siska/Lifesize/Getty Images; p. 15 Anonymous/The Bridgeman Art Library/Getty Images; pp. 16–17 Ryan Creary/All Canada Photos/Getty Images; p. 18 Glow Images, Inc/Glow/Getty Images; p. 19 Tom Merton/OJO Images/Getty Images; p. 20 Dimitrios/Shutterstock.com; p. 21 Comstock/Getty Images; p. 22 S0ulsurfing - Jason Swain/Flickr/Getty Images.

Library of Congress Cataloging-in-Publication Data

Berne, Emma Carlson.
Speeding! : mechanical energy / by Emma Carlson Berne. — 1st ed.
p. cm. — (Energy everywhere)
Includes index.
ISBN 978-1-4488-9651-6 (library binding) — ISBN 978-1-4488-9760-5 (pbk.) —
ISBN 978-1-4488-9761-2 (6-pack)
1. Motion—Juvenile literature. 2. Force and energy—Juvenile literature. 3. Power (Mechanics—Juvenile literature. I. Title.
QC127.4.B47 2013
531'.11—dc23

2012022319

Manufactured in the United States of America

CPSIA Compliance Information: Batch #W13PK4: For Further Information contact Rosen Publishing, New York, New York at 1-800-237-9932

CONTENTS

MATTER IN MOTION

Imagine that you are riding a giant roller coaster, thundering down a huge hill. You are experiencing mechanical energy.

Energy is the ability of a system to do work. Energy comes in forms such as sound, light, and heat.

A roller coaster in motion is an example of mechanical energy. The ride's engine works harder to pull the cars up the hill than down it. You will learn why in this book.

At some power plants, the mechanical energy from falling water is used to produce electricity.

This book will explore mechanical energy, the energy of **matter** in motion. This is the energy that an object has due to its motion or to the possible energy the object has, even when it is not moving.

RESTING OR MOVING?

Mechanical energy can exist in two different states. One state is **potential energy**. This is the motion an object can do, even though it might be at rest. For instance, picture a skateboard sitting at the top of a slope. The skateboard is not moving, so it has potential energy.

When this person lets go of the rubber band, the stored mechanical energy will be released and will send the rubber band flying across the room.

If someone pushes the skateboard down the slope, it has **kinetic energy**. Kinetic energy is the energy of motion itself. All objects in the world have either potential energy or kinetic energy.

The force this boy applies to his skateboard releases the kinetic energy of the skateboard's wheels.

MASS, MOTION, AND FORCE

You know that an engine makes a car go. The car and its engine are examples of **mass**, motion, and **force**. These are important ideas in understanding mechanical energy. Mass is the amount of matter an object has. Motion is movement. Force is the push or pull applied to mass. Force is what sets the mass in motion.

Imagine a car and its engine. Both the car and the engine have mass. When the engine is started, the movement of the engine supplies the force that sets the car in motion.

Racecars have less mass than the cars you see on the street every day. This makes it easier for them to reach high speeds.

SPEED AND MOTION

When you think about motion, the first thing you probably think about is speed. Speed is how fast an object is going, which is measured by how far it can travel during a certain period of time. For example, a pitcher might throw a fastball at a speed of 90 miles per hour (145 km/h).

High-speed trains like this one accelerate to speeds of around 140 miles per hour (225 km/h).

Police use tools to measure drivers' speed. They can tell if drivers are speeding up or slowing down. In science, acceleration refers to both speeding up and slowing down. In common usage, slowing down is called deceleration.

This means that if the ball could travel at that speed for 1 hour, it would travel 90 miles (145 km)!

Acceleration is a change in speed, either slowing down or speeding up. When a car's gas pedal is pressed, the car starts to pick up speed. It is accelerating!

MEASURES OF SPEED

Speed can be measured in different ways. In the United States, speed is measured in miles per hour. Most other countries in the world measure speed in kilometers per hour.

The speed of boats is measured in nautical miles per hour. Nautical miles per hour are also called knots. Planes and rockets often use a unit called a Mach number.

The knot as a measuring unit for boat speed got its name because the measurement was once done using a special knotted rope.

Jet airplanes like this F-16 can reach Mach 2, which is a speed of about 1,522 miles per hour (2,450 km/h). Mach 2 is two times the speed of sound!

This measures how fast a plane is flying compared to the speed of sound. Mach 1 is the speed of sound.

The fastest speed in the universe is the speed of light as measured in a **vacuum**. The speed of light is 186,282 miles per second (299,792 km/s)!

This speedometer shows both kilometers per hour (outside) and miles per hour (inside).

WHAT IS GRAVITY?

Gravity is the force that pulls all objects downward, toward the ground. Picture a roller coaster rolling down a hill. The roller coaster is being pulled downward by gravity.

Gravity is related to **inertia**. Inertia means that objects want to stay in the same state they are already in. If an object is at rest, it will stay at rest unless acted on by a force. Likewise, objects that are in motion will keep moving unless acted on by a force that will slow or stop their movement.

Gravity is the force that pulls you down a slide.

ISAAC NEWTON

Sir Isaac Newton was an English scientist who lived from 1642 until 1727. Newton was one of the first people to explain gravity and describe three key laws of motion.

FRICTION: SLOWING IT DOWN

If you are riding your bike and you begin going down a hill, the force of gravity will make you pick up speed. Have you ever thought about how a bike's brakes help you slow down or stop? That is **friction** at work. Friction is when one object rubs against another object. This action slows an object's movement.

If you look at a bike's brakes, you will see that they are little rubber pads on either side of the tire. When you use the brakes, these pads apply friction to the tire, slowing the speed at which the wheels are moving.

Besides the brakes, there is also friction between the bike's tires and the surface on which it is rolling. There is more friction between the tires and grass than between tires and a road.

POWER AND SIMPLE MACHINES

Simple machines are mechanical devices that change the direction or the **power** of a force. This multiplies the force and makes it possible to do tasks that would be very hard or impossible for you to do without the simple machine.

This crane is using the pulley located at the top to lift a box.

A car jack uses a simple machine called a lever. This makes it possible for one person to lift a car so that a tire can be changed.

One kind of simple machine is a pulley. A pulley is a wheel with a rope on its outside edge. To use a pulley, you might tie one end of a rope around a heavy box, thread it over the pulley, and pull on the other end. The pulley makes it easier for you to lift the heavy box.

CONVERTING MECHANICAL ENERGY

Sometimes, we can convert, or change, energy into other forms that are useful to us. A hand-cranked **generator** uses mechanical energy to create electrical energy, for example. The kinetic energy of your hands turning the crank is what powers this kind of generator.

Winding a clock stores the energy from the winding in a spring within the clock. As the spring unwinds, this stored energy becomes the mechanical energy that turns the gears that power the clock.

The food you eat is stored chemical energy. The release of this energy fuels your body, allowing you to run and do everything else your body does.

One of the most important rules of energy is that it cannot be created or destroyed. This is true no matter what form it is converted from or into. All of the energy in the universe is constantly being converted into other forms.

THE ENERGY OF MOTION

Mechanical energy is everywhere in your world. You can see it in a yellow school bus rumbling down the street, a baseball zooming over home plate, or a construction crane lifting a block of concrete. Even the flushing of your toilet in the bathroom is an example of mechanical energy.

As you go through your day, look for examples of your own. Without the energy of motion, our world would be a still, silent place.

On a seesaw, you use mechanical energy to move up and down. The seesaw is a combination of two simple machines that make moving loads easier. They are the lever and the fulcrum.

GLOSSARY

acceleration (ik-SEH-luh-ray-shun) How much faster something moves once it starts moving.

force (FORS) Something that moves or pushes on something else.

friction (FRIK-shin) The rubbing of one thing against another.

generator (JEH-neh-ray-tur) A machine that makes electricity.

inertia (ih-NER-shuh) The law that says that matter will stay at rest unless a force acts upon it and that matter will stay in motion unless a force acts upon it.

kinetic energy (kuh-NEH-tik EH-nur-jee) The energy of motion.

mass (MAS) The amount of matter in something.

matter (MA-ter) Anything that has weight and takes up space.

potential energy (puh-TEN-shul EH-nur-jee) Work that a thing might do.

power (POW-er) The ability to have an effect on something else.

simple machines (SIM-pel muh-SHEENZ) Devices that change the direction or power of a force.

vacuum (VA-kyoom) A space that is empty of air or any other matter.

INDEX

WEBSITES

Due to the changing nature of Internet links, PowerKids Press has developed an online list of websites related to the subject of this book. This site is updated regularly. Please use this link to access the list: www.powerkidslinks.com/enev/speed/